# ANIMALS

# WITH

# TINY

# CAT

## Viviane Schwarz

**WALKER BOOKS**
AND SUBSIDIARIES
LONDON • BOSTON • SYDNEY • AUCKLAND

# CAT

This Walker book
belongs to:

_____

_____

_____

To Christina and Tiger

First published 2018 by Walker Books Ltd,
87 Vauxhall Walk, London SE11 5HJ

This edition published 2020

2 4 6 8 10 9 7 5 3 1

British Library Cataloguing in Publication Data:
a catalogue record for this book is
available from the British Library

ISBN 978-1-4063-8160-3

www.walker.co.uk

# MOUSE

# ELEPHANT

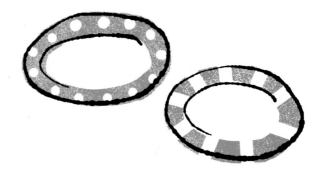

# BIRD

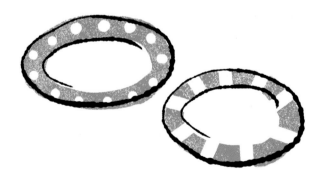

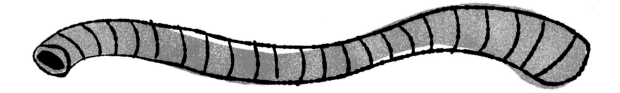

# HORSE

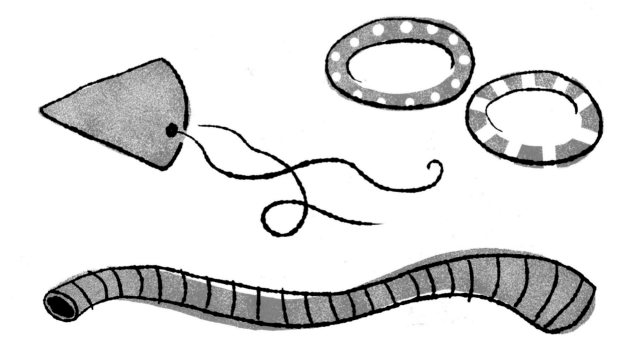

# PORCUPINE

SNUFFLE

# SNAKE

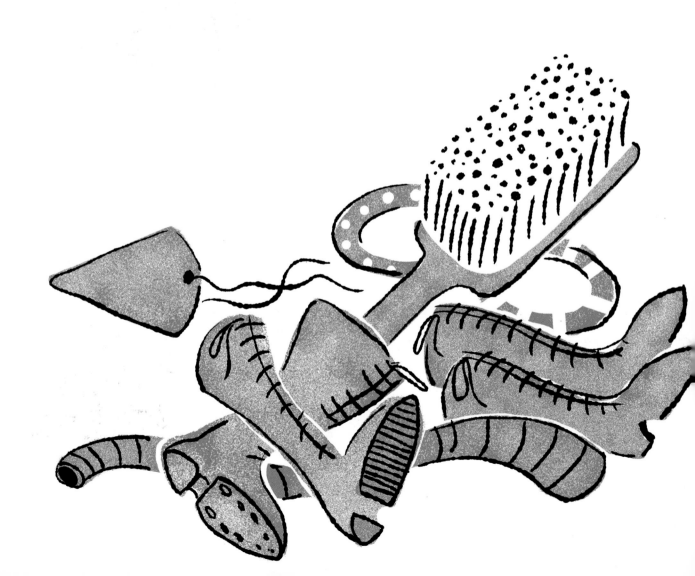

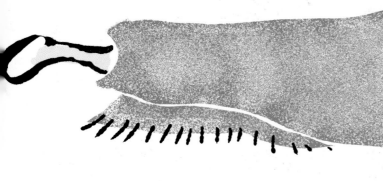

# SPIDER

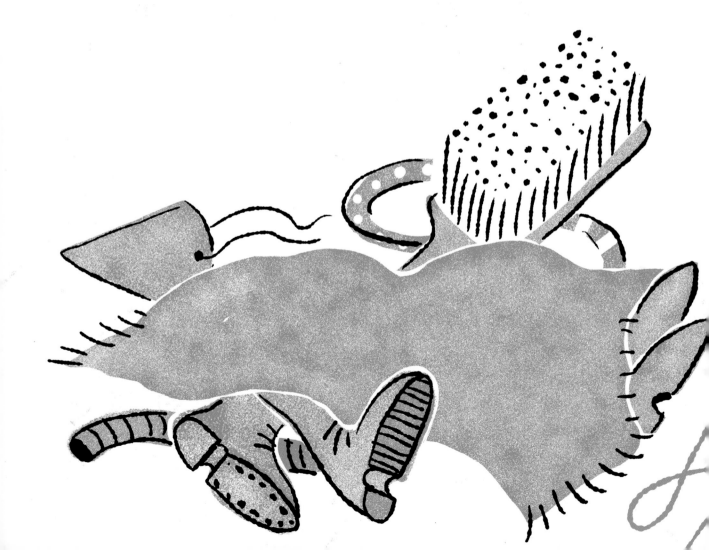

# DRAGON

# LION!

# Look out for:

There are cats in this book

Viviane Schwarz

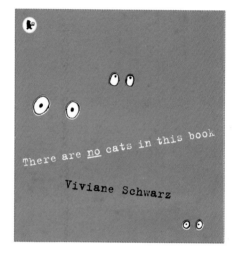

There are <u>no</u> cats in this book

Viviane Schwarz

"Witty, original and charming"
*The Sunday Times*

A *Publishers Weekly*
Best Book of the Year

978-1-4063-2499-0

"A clever, interactive read"
*Herald*

Shortlisted for the
Kate Greenaway Medal

978-1-4063-3102-8

Is there a
dog in this
book?

Viviane Schwarz

Winner of the Children's Book Award

"A hilarious romp"
*The New York Times*

978-1-4063-6090-5

Available from all good booksellers  www.walker.co.uk